D1652090
T5-CCF-442

The Story of

Digby *and* Marie

Robert Shure

Illustrations by

Ajla S. Selenic

St. Martin's Press
New York

A THOMAS DUNNE BOOK.
An imprint of St. Martin's Press.

THE STORY OF DIGBY AND MARIE.

Design by Peter M. Blaiwas, Vernon Press, Inc.

ISBN 0-312-15011-3

First Edition: May 1997
10 9 8 7 6 5 4 3 2 1

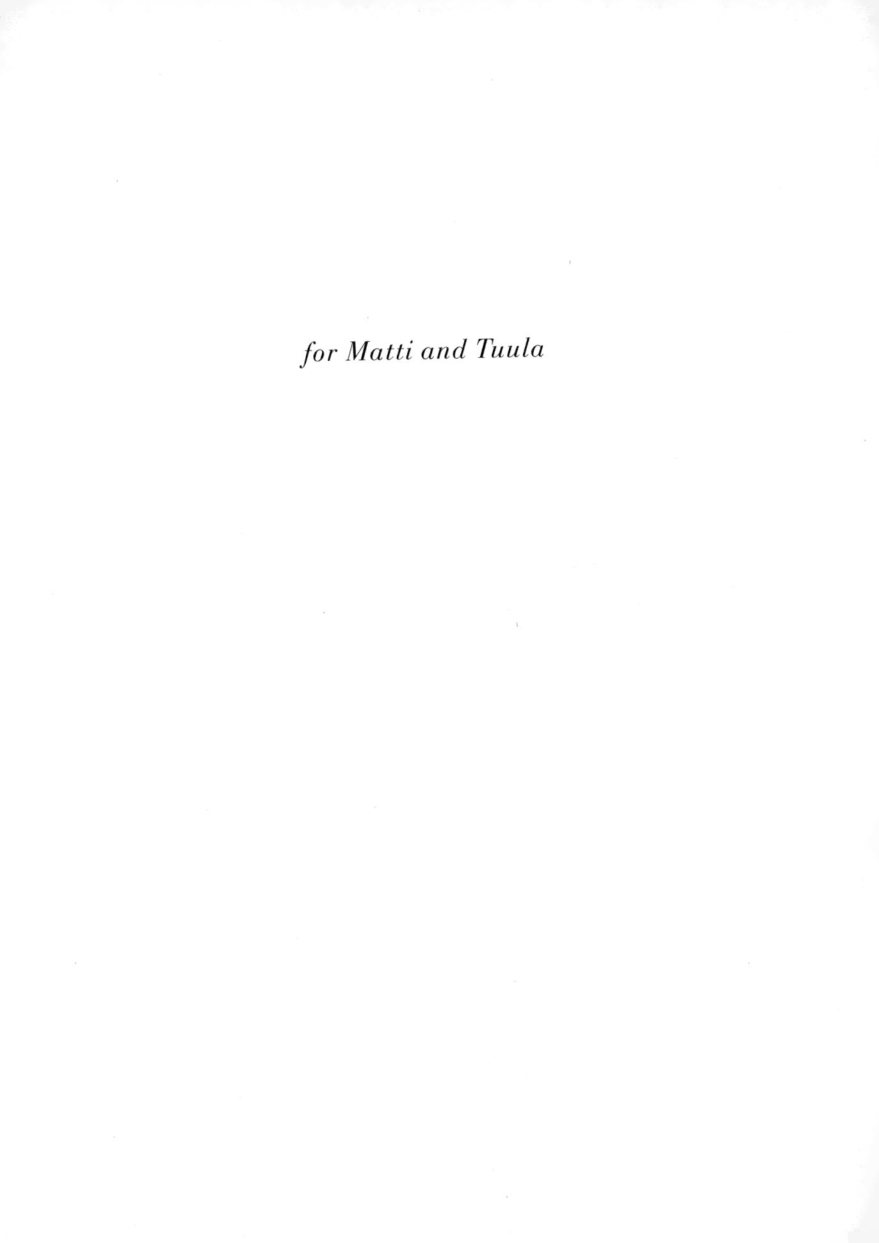

for Matti and Tuula

Do you speak to strangers?

Body language is my native tongue.

Say something in it.

Well maybe...just this.

Is that a complete sentence?

It's a simple question.
I'm waiting for an answer.

I don't know the language.

There's nothing to it.
A noun is always made in the eyes,
a verb in the hips,
an adjective in one or both legs.

How do I know which noun?

In body language, there's only one noun.

There is?

It's just that it's said in so many ways.

What about verbs?

Several are known...
each phrased by precisely what
one does with the hips.

And the adjectives?
Each phrased by what one does
with the legs?

Well of course taste enters into it.

And what of the rest of me?

What about it?

For example, what's the
stomach used for?

Dangling participles.

And the posterior?

Body slang. Which I disapprove of.
Well? Stand up and try it.

Uh...how's this?

Look at you. What happened to you?

I believe the trouble has
come from within.

How so?

My moral fiber
is being eaten away.

What by?

Lust, in small quantities.

Who for?

A slithering figure
I thought I'd forgotten.

Who was she, exactly?

I have no idea.
There was someone half-hidden
in shadows one time.
I never could get a look at the rest.

So?

Late these nights,
I've been dwelling on that half of her.

What if you found her?

I'd politely inquire as to
whether or not she might be agreeable
to a mild form of perverse activity.

If the answer is yes?

If at all possible, I'll deal
directly with that half of her
that I know so well.

If the answer is no?

I might look into the half I don't.

Meanwhile, what are you
planning to do with yourself?

I've decided to lose my mind
for a week.

Instead of what?

Just going on like this,
day after day.

The question is,
is it worth all the trouble?

By and large, it's going to be a real
adventure.

You think so?

I'll laugh when I want to laugh,
not when I have to.

And cry, I suppose.

I can go up to strangers
right on the street, and be as warm
and friendly as I choose.

I used to do that...when I was insane.

We could go together.

No thanks. My lunatic days are behind me.

What were they like?

I was hated for being so loving.

Tell me about it.

I'd meet someone new,
and throw myself into him.
Crawl through his psyche
and swim through his soul.

That's loving, all right.

And all I got was a sneer in return.

I wonder why.

Sad to say, when it comes to passion,
hysterics have gone out of style.

Everything worthwhile somehow has.

My derangement was totally wasted.

I suppose mine would be too.

I just don't think
you'd get anything out of it,
except grief and misery.

What a pity.

Well, sanity does have its own rewards.

Such as?

A little serenity.
I can meet someone new now,
and remain in control.

Even someone who
speaks your language?

I think you just spoke it.

What did I say?

You wouldn't know.

I think what I'll do is just
lose my mind for a second or two.

Go right ahead.

And when I get back?

I'll be waiting.

I once sold chest wigs to bashful men.

How was business?

Beyond expectations.
I could hardly keep up with demand.

An invaluable service.
It must have been deeply rewarding.

That's hard to remember.
It was so long ago.

I know.

Excuse me?

Through some retail outlet,
I was one of your customers.
Here. Take a look.

As a matter of fact,
that wasn't my brand.

You simply don't recognize it.
I've had it modified over the years.

For what purpose?

I thought it should fit my changing needs.
With self-confidence, for example,
I had it trimmed down.

The business went bad
as we entered
the age of self-expression.
When the men insisted
on growing their own.

That must have been after my time.

Still, I thought it was
something worth doing.
It was back when I wanted
to find who I was, and
just what my talents might be.

And?

One of them, it turned out,
was a knack for discovering
a weakness in others,
and preying on those weaknesses
for personal gain.

In other words, you found
you possessed
a keen business sense.

But the question is,
looking back, what good did it do?

It put some hair on my chest.

Did you hear that?

I know that bird.
He sings off-key.

They think they have talent.
Some don't.

Whenever I'm out here,
it's the same old song
and the same dumb mistakes.

They're like that.

Yesterday, as soon as he
started I quickly joined in,
with all the corrections.

Did it do any good?

He just drowned me out,
with those hideous notes.

Try and ignore him.

It's not that easy.

What do you mean?

I don't know,
there's something about him.

What, exactly?

I suppose in a way...
I can see myself in that sad
little creature.

What do you see?

To begin with,
when I first heard him sing,
he wasn't that bad.

So?

Since that time, it so happens
I've seen him poking around
with various females of the species.
And the truth of it is,
they've ruined him.

Is that what happened to you?

Well just look at me.
Listen to me.

The question is, what were
you like when you started out?

Somebody else.
You wouldn't have known me.

I only hope...someone
like me can't cause further damage.

It simply happens.
It's beyond your control.

In which case,
I suppose I should leave.

I suppose.

And what if
there's never anyone else?

Maybe that's what I need.

What you're going to need...
what you always did...
is a soul somewhere, with whom
to share something in common.

True.

And if no one's around?

There's the bird.

Think hard.
Isn't there somebody? Somewhere?

What about you?
Wife? Mother?

I was no good at childbirth.
When the time came,
I just left him
in there.

A son?

So to speak.

What happened?

He found his own way,
a week later.

And then?

From the very beginning,
he treated me as a total stranger.

How did you handle him?

For his own good,
I let him go free.

Didn't you feel empty and sad?

We weren't right for each other.
We both knew that.

Have you seen him since?

He's been very busy and so have I,
but we've squeezed in some lunches
over the years.

How is he?

He's still angry at me.
He says his birthday
should be a week earlier.

But what is he like?

He's me in a man.
All I could want,
if you know what I mean.

But I've made no overtures.
That's not who I am.

And what's to become of him?
Or wouldn't you know?

If genes mean anything, I know.

What?

He'll live out his life in a dreamlike state,
yearning for more than is really there.

I suppose it's possible...
we have something in common.

I suppose.

Digby's the name.

Marie.

It's Spring again...
and time for my sunbathing stencils.

What good do they do?

Tan words on my body send a message.

Saying what?

Containing clues to the inner me.

For example.

Come out to the beach
and read me some time.

Why be like that,
around all those strangers?

On these carefree warm days, I love
the freedom of exposing myself. My real self.

I suppose you attract lots of attention.

Last year, a pale gentleman was so moved
by my words that he stood
there in tears.

And?

A week later, he was back
with a lovely brown message of his own.

Was that the end of it?

I had more to tell, and so did he.
A week would go by, and another part
of him spelled out some secret.
Then another week, and a
new part of me would.

So?

We never spoke, that man and I,
but we knew each other inside out.

I have to keep my
personal messages to myself.

What for?

I don't tan.

There's no harm in my coming here...
but I'll have to maintain my other connections.

And the same can be said,
it so happens, for me.
As I stated previously...
I have a certain half-woman in mind.

Of course. Anyway, as for today,
I have an engagement.

You'll notice I'm not asking for details.

If you must know,
I've been invited to the Wine Tasters Ball.

Who by?

The chairman himself.
He's asked me for pointers
on the art of human compassion.
That's my field. That's what I do.

Do for who?

People in need, from all walks of life.

They ask you for that?

They seek me out.
Actually, his whole organization could use me.

Wine tasters?

A tragic bunch.

Oh?

Beyond their tongues,
sensual pleasure is totally unknown to them.

But they're having that Ball.
They must enjoy that.

They dance without bending their elbows.
It keeps them apart, which is
just how they like it.

Wasted lives.

I know what to do, to people like that.

Maybe some day, you can do it to me.

How about the wine taster?

When I finished with him, he was bending both elbows. Flushed with feelings, there on the dance floor. His cheeks were all damp.

How did you do it?

I'm better than wine.

And what about me?

I need to know more.

About what, exactly?

Tell me a little about yourself.
Who you are, that sort of thing.

Well...going back...way back...
I've always felt...I was
part of a multiple birth.

With a secret twin?

Two other triplets. I just close
my eyes and there they are,
one on each side of me.

Doing what?

Staring in horror. I'm the crude one.

You're the only one.

Tell that to them.

Crude how?

By comparison, that's how. They
turned out right. Charming. Irresistible.

Oh?

They make me feel ashamed.
I was meant to be born like him,
or like him. But look what came out.

Are they really so wonderful?

They're me, in the
proper form.

If I were you, I'd simply get rid of them.

You can't be serious.

The question is, which one is here?
If it's really you,
I'd prefer your being you, as you.

Me? Do you mean that?

I think it's time you opened your eyes.

Wait. They're still closed, and look!
They're gone! And maybe...just maybe...
you can take her place.

Whose place?

That half a woman.

I think you should know...something about me. It so happens...I wear a mask.

Of who?

Of me. My face appears on a mask I wear.

Are you wearing it now?

No, but that was it yesterday.

And the day before?

No, that was me.

It must be an exact likeness.

It is now. But I'm thinking of later.

How much later?

When I'll want to look like my old self again.

When will that be?

As soon as I notice there's two of me.

Have you done this before?

I have a new mask made every so often.

Why bother?

Whether we see it or not,
we're deteriorating minute by minute.
I don't like that.

That's understandable.

I simply decided to put a stop to it.

But we do fall apart, sooner or later.

I'd rather decay in occasional chunks
than constantly, bit by bit.

Tell me more.

More about what?

You. What you are.
Where you've been.

Well...I was once committed
to a home for incurable romantics.

Committed by whom?

Someone disgusted
by the thrill of my touch.

Did she know what she was letting you in for?

Not until visitors' day. She was shocked by
the rules that were strictly enforced.

Such as?

Residents could never gather in pairs.

Cruel.

Still, the hardened romantics would manage
somehow. Outbreaks of passion took place
in steam vents, and crawl spaces, and once
in an abandoned hot water tank.

That one sounds beautiful.

That one was me.

How did it end?

The lady and I were caught,
and dealt with. I got off easy.
Solitary confinement.

And the lady?

It so happened, she was one of the staff.
An obedience trainee. A reformed romantic
who regressed at the sight of me.

What did they do to her?

Vicious punishment. They forced her
onto an all-starch diet.

No.

It completely destroyed the rest of her life.

Whatever became of her?

She slowly turned into
a practicing psychologist.

Poor thing.

Her sensual side was entirely erased.
Romantically speaking, she was
never heard from again.

A tragic story.

One of many.

Things happen to us, beyond our control.

I know. I've got moles all over me.

Caused by what.

A sad love, in each case.
Whenever it happens, I grow a mole.

Are they all very dark?

Some darker than others.
Depends on the woman.

Do they hurt?

Only while forming.
After a while I'm basically numb.

That's good.

Until the next one.

Maybe you should just stop falling in love.

I tried that once.

What happened?

In the presence of women,
I covered my eyes, cupped my ears
and wore steel wool gloves.

Well?

Her distinctive aroma penetrated deep.

And?

She's the one here on the knuckle.

So much love.
Must have left you with memories.

It's left me with moles. And you?

Fat deposits.

Where, by and large?

Generally speaking,
over all this and under all that.

And caused by just what?

Each love, as a rule, would bring on some fat.

So that's what causes it.

In the interim I'd thin out.
But then there I'd go again.

But why, I wonder.

In sensitive people such as myself,
heartfelt feelings tend to soften
bodily tissue, allowing for
fatty buildup.

I hadn't heard that.

It's a known phenomenon.
And potentially a dangerous one...
considering what else can result.

What else?

Little miseries that can start to seep in.

Are you trying to say that love
can be dangerous?

Wouldn't you?

Well, it leaves its mark. I'll say that.

The question is...are you growing a mole over me?

I beg your pardon?

Maybe it's just a freckle at this point.

Oh, listen. Under normal circumstances...
you'd be a noticeable splotch by now. As it
happens, however...

Yes?

...I'm preoccupied at present...
as I have been for months...
by memories of a certain half-woman.

So?

Deep into the night...
I start filling in the other half.

Well start erasing.
Your mind isn't big enough for the two of us.

Wait a minute.
Are you trying to say...
that you're really interested here?

It's business. I'm conducting an experiment,
during which time you have to be
concentrating on no one but me.

What's the point?

I want to determine how long it takes
for a woman like me to excite a lost soul.

And how would you do that, exactly?

I wouldn't tell.
It would kill the experiment.

And what if it fails completely?

Then something is wrong with you.

It could be the experimenter.

You really think so?

It's possible...
there's just not that much to her.

And just how much of a woman
might it take to excite you?

Maybe half.

I just remembered my very first thought.

When was that?

Back in the cradle. It suddenly
struck me that my toes were
lined up according to height.

Still something to think about.

I wondered why the fingers weren't.
And that's when I realized
that some things just weren't
going to turn out right.

I knew that the moment I appeared.

You did?

I'll never forget the reception I got.
Their first concern was something
extremely private.

Well, sure. There's one thing
they're eager to know right
from the start.

The wrong thing.
It so happened I was crying like crazy.
But no one cared why.

I know the feeling.

I could sense right away just what I was in for.

This brings back a bleak period
in my life. Up to now, I've been able
to block most of it out.

Sometimes it's good to dig these things up.

The worst part of all was that sense
of helplessness. Muscle groups void.
Hand-eye coordination a joke.

Very unfortunate.

No doubt, psychologically,
it left me with scars.
A lack of self-confidence.
A deep-seated feeling of no-can-do.

It's a shame we're so weak
when it matters the most.

I realize now I'm a functional failure.

That's really too bad.

Pitiful, I'd say.

Well at least you know why.

I guess this is known as
self-discovery.

Let's dig some more.
Try and think hard. What else
was really horrible back then?

What's the point?

More self-discovery.
You might be more pitiful than you thought.

I have an appointment. I'm speaking to fitness
instructors this morning. Poor things.
They're pathetic, all right. But I can help them.

What about the fitness instructors?

We met in a lecture hall.
Each one of them came in alone,
ignoring the others.

What happened?

I began by describing what I knew
they were missing...the emotional life,
the sensuous fulfillment...and they started
to squirm...perspiring noticeably...

Go on.

Soon I went into graphic details,
and the more I went into,
the more they perspired.
Those tank tops were soaking.

Then what?

At the crucial moment, I commended them
on their splendid achievements...

those magnificent lumps all over their bodies...
which were going to waste...on display,
yes, but ungrazed, unfondled, uncherished...

And then?

In a minute or two they were
out of control, gyrating right there
in their seats. When they finally calmed down,
they began strolling out in tightly knit pairs,
not many lumps still unattended.

I can only imagine...
it's safe to assume...
that you yourself used
to stroll that way.

Sad to say,
people didn't have lumps in those days.

Looking back,
the most passionate men
were the dentists.

Well, that's what they're known for.

You could see it in their eyes,
the moment you sat down.

Same with the women.
I used to fake toothaches for love.

I wonder what makes them
these sensual creatures.

In dental school, they're taught
that pain can be pleasure. And,
well, they're made to feel that,
which gets them aroused, and
eager to pass it along.

They did it superbly, in my case.
The last one, especially.

Why not go back?

He'd have nothing to do.

Well, you can always lie down
with your memories.

I've done that.
And it just makes me feel
that my life's incomplete.

Well maybe...in time...
I can do something about that.

Yes, perhaps that's what I'm missing.
The passion of pain.

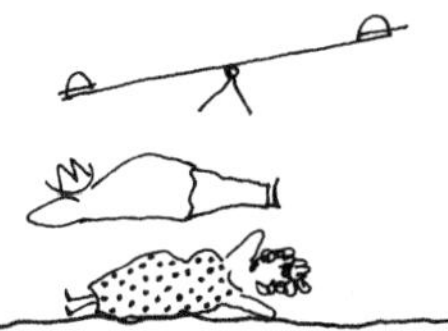

I hypnotize myself
on weekends.

Employing which method?

The face-in-the-mirror
technique.

Which works basically how?

I simply sit there and gaze
at myself, until I'm in total control.

You must cast a powerful signal.

Well, I've perfected the art.

Think of the chance to influence people.

Unfortunately, it doesn't
work on anyone else.

Exactly how does it work on you?

I utter a couple of random commands,
and believe me, I'm quick to obey.

Commands to do what, for example?

Oh, reveal my innermost
feelings about something. Someone.

You need to be hypnotized,
just to think of your feelings?

They're buried too deep.
I don't know what they are.

Let's find out. Here, I have a mirror.

Oh...no...see, it's only Wednesday.
On off-days, sometimes it doesn't
work at all. Sometimes I get distracted.

By what?

Well, for one thing...

Yes?

All right, I'll give it a try,
and see what happens.

Go right ahead.

Uh...hello there. Now. Just relax. That's it.
All right, you're growing...tired...more
tired...more. In a couple of seconds...you're
going to be out. Just...out. There. Now...
just what are you feeling today? Hmm?
What...and for whom...and how much?

Well?

I ask again...What are you
feeling...and...and...

Go on. Go on.

What are you actually...?
That face...those eyes...

What's the matter with you? Why aren't you answering? Why are you only gazing like that?

I can't help it.

Why not?

I'm spellbound.

That...was deep. I may never have been...
that far in.

I'd like to know...
what feelings you found there.

Strange...I wouldn't call it a feeling as
such...but it seems there was something...
with you involved.

Me? What, exactly? What was it?

I don't know, for a second or two...
I believe you were flashing before me.

Then what?

You just faded out.

But obviously, I'm having an effect.

Meaning what, I wonder.

Perhaps we'll find out, after dinner tomorrow.

* *

My eyes are changing color again.

How often does it happen?

It used to be once every four years.
But now it's once every three.

So the process is speeding up a bit.

I think I know why.

It's probably age.
More sensitive to light
as the years go on.

It's not the light. It's the mind.

Well. One or the other.

Mentally, I go in cycles.
Every third year now, I tend to feel
that I'm somebody else,
with different thrills, a different sadness,
attracted to a whole different person.

I can't say the same.

This, of course, alters certain organic functions. Heart rate, nerve sensitivity, factors of physical pigmentation.

Does your hair color change?

No, that's controllable. Eyes are not.

Maybe it doesn't matter that much.

On the contrary. Clothes make the man, eyes make the woman.

Well how have you seen yourself
through your own eyes?

Essentially...sultry in brown,
coy in dark green,
a little more daring in blue.

And right now?

I'll leave that to you.

Oh. Well. From what I can see...
right at this moment...there's a certain...
brownish...dark greenish...
blue.

Really?

Whatever that means.

I think what it means...
is that now what you're seeing...
is in reality...just who I am.

Then that's...in reality...just who you are.

For another three years.

Excuse me a moment.

I beg your pardon?

I've been waiting to do this, with <u>someone</u>.

Do what?

Show you...a certain something here.

A certain what?

Well, you see...

Yes?

This grape is a family heirloom.

Since when?

My great-grandfather traced it to ancient times. It seems it survived an orgy.

Oh?

A slave girl dropped it in an emperor's mouth, but he spit it back out at her.

I wonder why.

He was making a statement. She hadn't pleased him the night before. At least that's what she wrote when she buried it.

What made her do that?

A sense of history. Centuries later, that's what a countess told my great-grandfather, as she slipped it into his palm.

Then what?

He was overcome by raw emotion,
and swore he would keep it close
to his heart. But she ditched him in the
morning, and he started to squash it.
Look, you can still see the scar.

What happened then?

He did keep it, and then on his
deathbed bequeathed it to his
daughter, my grandmother,
a bitter man still. "When you grow up,"
he told her, "give it to someone you
don't give a damn for. Let <u>him</u> get all
excited for nothing."

And?

Years later she gave it to my
grandfather. They were married
by then and she couldn't stand him.
The fact is, he knew that, but
still he accepted it sentimentally.
Do you know why? Because that's
how he was. And he's the one
I take after.

Oh...go on...

Well he in turn passed it on to
his daughter, my mother, who
gave it to me. And she said:
"See what it does for you, my son.
It might bring you luck. I hope so.
You'll need it."

I'd have loved your mother.

And that, pretty much, is the
story of the grape.

Touching.

And now...I'd like you to have it.

Me? Oh, I couldn't.

No, go right ahead. It's only fitting.
Think of all that it's meant.

Well, if you really insist. Oh it does feel...
the question is, where will I...? Wait.
Where did it go? Oh here it is.
Flat under my shoe.

It is?

<u>Very</u> flat, I'm afraid.

Oh?

Well, it must not have been...
as hard as it used to be.

Yes...some things harden...
then soften with age.

What a sad little ending.

Sad but true.

Fortunately, along the way
it did give some pleasure.

That's what a grape is for.

The absolute worst morning of my career!
As a group, they're hopeless!
Beyond any help! All the writers
wanted to do was handle me!
Not listen to me! Not gain any insights
about what it is that makes them pathetic!
Loveless degenerates! Well that's what
they are and that's what they'll be!
That's what the writers will always be!
Oh, afterwards, a few had some manners.
Talking, smiling. The nonfiction ones.
But the novelists grabbed me,
panting and moaning, while the poets
were deviously poking around!

I'm having a ghostwriter do my diary.

So he told me. In a more interesting way.

The fact is, I'm tired of all this
monotonous drivel. I want to
read of exciting days and
meaningful nights. I want to see
some spice in my life.

And what about the personal things?
What about me?

Believe me...rereading these pages,
I think your dialogue could use some
improvement.

And what about you?
What if he misses the real person?

That's been my problem.

And just who do you think you really might be?

Good question. And starting
right here, right on this page,
I hope to find out.

Oh?

At least I know...that this much is me.
Arms...legs...spinal column...

A good deal of nothing, when the time comes.

Not necessarily.
When the funeral's over,
I'm having my bones recycled.

What for?

It's a way I can last through the ages...
in people's dishes, ash trays, book ends...

Not that memorable.

On the other hand, I might simply
go on display, as is. Allow medical
students to study my structure.

I don't think they'd use you.

Why not?

The students aren't meant to
feel pity for skeletons.

Meaning what?

Your framework is something less than ideal.

So?

You'll be better off as recycled material.

I'm sending love letters
to thousands of strangers.

Most people don't read their junk mail.

If I get just ten answers,
it'll be a success.

Answers to what?

The simple question...
how can I make you a happy woman?

What's the point?

I need some ideas. To use on you.

Why not just ask me what makes me happy?

I thought it would be nice
if I could just try and do it,
without having to ask.

Go right ahead.

Well first, I'd like to check with
the public at large. I might get some
really beautiful thoughts...
if I asked in this personal
and intimate way.

You think so?

Let's see if they answer.

You've never asked me in a personal way.
Intimate either.

Well...then maybe...just maybe...
I ought to do that.

Maybe you ought to.

I think I'm ready. Ready right now.

Good. Mail it in the morning.
Let's see if I answer.

* *

As you'll notice...in my self-portrait,
the face is hidden.

Interesting technique.

What I mean to convey
is a deep-seated modesty.

I'd say it succeeds on all levels.

It's not easy. As I work,
I can't let myself look in a mirror.

Well, self-discipline
is a virtue in an artist.

Now study it closely,
and say what you think.
I want the truth.

I have to keep telling myself
that it's you.

That's the beauty of art. It conveys
what real life doesn't.

Your modesty, for example. In real life,
I might never have caught it.

Think of what else about me
you just might be missing.

Well, I hope you keep painting yourself.

I intend to. Next time,
I'm going to hide my whole body.

Are you really concerned with
making me happy?

Pardon me?

I do have a problem. Perhaps you can help.

What kind of problem?

Deep in my mind, all my
dead lovers are competing for space.

Well, what I'd say is...
get rid of a few.

I do all the time.
But they keep slipping back.

You may have to be a little more vicious.

I've already used some brutal techniques.

Such as.

Oh, turning one's face into somebody else's.

Not brutal enough.

And sometimes, I'll let one of my
favorites pound another one,
until nothing is left.

Not bad.

Until it's <u>his</u> turn.

Still not enough.

What can I do?

There's a foolproof way
to eliminate one.

What's that?

Well...what you do is...
just bring him to mind...

Yes?

...think of him, and think hard...

And then?

Black out.

That's vicious.

I've done it with live ones. It works every time.

I actually think there is something here. Something between us.

If I just weren't obsessed
by that certain half...

Think of her. And black out.

Oh I can't, in her case.
She might still be alive.

So?

I just keep wondering...
what she's doing right now.
And what I could be doing...
along with her.

Take the half you don't know...
and simply think of it...as that half of me.

Say...that does kind of give
you another dimension.

Meaning what, exactly?

I do believe...I could come
to feel deeply...for a good part of you.

Maybe some day, you'll deserve the rest.

I've been taking my baths
in sparkling water.

You do look refreshed.

I'm invigorated, inside and out.
I have a new zest for living.

It shows.

That includes...uh...certain friendly
desires. If you know what I mean.

I wouldn't be interested.
It so happens, I've been bathing in vinegar.

What for?

It's a wonderful preservative.
Too bad it just happens to leave me drained.

What's the point of preserving yourself,
if there's no excitement?

I'm devoting the rest of the year to my skin.

What's the point?

I don't want to look in the mirror one day,
and see some rumpled-up hag.

I'd rather be rumpled
and have a great year.

There'll be other years.

Actually, I think I have
the solution to this.

I doubt it.

You could add sparkling water
to your bath next time.
And I'll add some vinegar to mine.

For what purpose?

Well, you know. The two of us.
Your tub or mine.

Thanks all the same.

I don't think you get the idea here.
You might say...we could sparkle together.

I'd just as soon be drained alone.

A tragic thought, if I ever heard one.

The tragedy is, being a hag in a mirror.

The tragedy is...
being invigorated for nothing.

I notice you're trashing your
personal effects.

They're not me. I'm somebody new now.

Due to what?

A serious career move.
It's all arranged. Next week,
I start teaching my specialty in the schools.

What for?

I want those young minds.

For what purpose?

To begin with, we need
a more sensual population.

You really think so?

Most days, I'll be right in the classroom.

While I do what?

I've assigned you a role there.

Me?

You can tell them how,
in our very own case, compassion
just came out of nowhere.

When was that?

I was thinking of next Sunday,
near the end of dinner.

This coming Sunday?

We can stare at each other a minute
or two, let some blood rush around,
and then have our dessert.

So you want to do that before
your first lesson.

I would not teach compassion
without an experience fresh in my mind.

I get up and dance during my dreams.

What for?

I don't know. It's beyond my control.

Are you dancing alone?

As far as I know.

How about in the dreams?

There's usually somebody.

And who might that be?

Possibly you, in some form or other.

And what do we do,
when the dance finally ends?

The dance never ends.

Maybe sometime, the dream
can come true.

What good would that do?

I might learn something.

Why bother?

Some night, I might
have a dream of my own.

*

You know...I look at you,
here in the dark, and I see
a life-size negative.

Tell me more.

I have to admit, the effect
is breathtaking.
The soft white eyeballs...

And?

The teeth with that
luscious black glow...

What else?

Overall, you're not you.
You're just the opposite.

What would you call me?

I'd have to say...
a bewitching creature.

*You've never talked to me
like this before.*

You've never been like this before.

Oh?

Pardon me for saying this, but...

I believe this may be what is known
as contentment.

Really?

Yes. And there's only one problem.

What?

Well, I've known such
contentment, and it's always led
to some sort of trouble.

What kind of trouble?

Heartbreak and sorrow.
And, to be perfectly frank,
I can't let that happen again.

Meaning?

Meaning...I'm afraid I'll have
to do something drastic.

Namely what?

Namely...
get rid of it right at its source.

And do what?

Just...this.

A flashlight. How could you?

My body fluids are evaporating.

It's the air these days.
It's sucking us dry.

My natural juices are down to nothing.

And my membranes are parched.
I can feel it.

I can't cry over it. I have no tears.

I've even lost the water in my knee.

What can we do?

Relief could be coming.
The scientists are at work.

The scientists? Speaking of people
who need my services...

They're accomplishing
the miraculous. People get what
they dream of. An injection of elegance.
A funny-bone implant.

When will they finally get around to us?

That's the question. So far,
they haven't considered anything
about us as truly significant.

My juices are gone!
How much more significant can you get?

Unfortunately, in those circles,
we're still thought of as out of
the mainstream.

In other words, they'll just let us rot.

We're thought of as throwaways.
We don't really matter.

Why is that? What is it about us?

They don't understand us.
Our sensitivities are too great.

Our passions too strong.

Our feelings too deep.

Maybe that's why...
too soon...we wear out.

Maybe that's why...
too soon...we dry up.

My memories of infancy
are fading fast.

What do you still remember the most?

My speech deficiency.
So much to say, no way to say it.

Same with me.

Well, it might not have mattered.
They were all concerned with the nose,
the chin, the eyes, etcetera.
Not the ideas.

Those asinine noises
they made with their mouths.
As if that was really my language.

The trouble being, there was
no one around to communicate with.

Actually, in my case there was.
In the park every day, I was put beside
another poor soul, about my age.
We were buggy to buggy. He babbled too,
but through it all we did
understand one another.

Wait a minute. Now that I think of it,
I had someone like that.

We aired out our problems together.
We knew just what was on each other's minds.

Sure. Same with me.

I gave my friend some useful advice.
At least I tried to.

What kind of advice?

Just an idea that worked for me.
That the next time his people
annoyed him like that, he could try drooling
on them. They just might back off.

Excellent idea.

I did my best to get it across.
Unfortunately, to do it,
I had to drool all over him.

I doubt if he minded.

He never minded, whatever I did.
Of all the relationships...through all the years...
that was the one that meant most to me.

Really?

I never knew what became of him.
I don't even know if he tried my idea.

He tried it.

What?

And it worked to perfection.

Do you mean to say...that was you?

So that...was you.

You've changed.
Well...I suppose I have too.

You're the same inside. I can tell.

I...I always wondered...
if I ever found him, what I would do.

I wondered that too.

Maybe...as long as it's us...
we don't have to do anything.

Probably not. But I think...
some kind of simple tender expression
on my part would be fitting.

If you like.

I have some ideas.

Go right ahead.

So much to say...no way to say it.

That sunset is leaking.

So I notice.

Now those colors will smear up
the whole West.

It's a small price to pay,
for the beauty we've seen.

But think of the mess that's coming.

It's only a sunset. We don't have to look.

Well what if we wanted to go
and fade into it? There we'd be,
dripping in orange and maroon.

I'd love that.

The whole experience would
be ruined. The whole adventure
I've been hoping for.

You have?

I thought it would be the perfect
way for us to wind up.

You and me, fading into the sunset?

Just imagine it.

*The question is, what would we do
when we got there?*

Normally, you just lie around,
and get these exotic sensations.

Let's go.

But look how sloppy
it's gotten now. Believe me,
it wouldn't be pleasant.

How could that happen?

It must have started with the sun
turning into that shapeless blob.

Well, we can always look East,
and wait for a whole new beginning.

You think so?

A simple sun, coming up clean.

By the time it gets West,
<u>that</u> might happen, all over again.

There'll be another one after that.

I'll say one thing. If it ever really does turn out right, think how stupendous...But all this waiting, and hoping, and wondering...

Let's take a look at the moon.

Well, finally, they've assigned
the stars to new constellations.

Who's up there now?

More up-to-date heroes.
Football greats. Matinee idols.

I'm not surprised.

That cluster off to the north,
for example. That's the box-office
king kissing you-know-who,
in a scene from their current smash.

A commercial sky.

There's a great action shot just above
the horizon. There. That's
what's-his-name scoring a winner.

No poets? No painters?

Oh, there's one particular
poetic soul. That's him straight up,
with the twinkling eye.

I don't see him.

That string of stars that curve at the end.
It's a nose you should recognize.

Oh?

And the chin. A familiar shape,
to say the least. Something you see...
day in and day out.

Are you trying to tell me that's you?

I applied. They said Yes.

On the basis of what? Who are <u>you</u>?

They wanted an everyday Man
for the Ages. And I happen
to have that look.

*What you're telling me is,
on all the clear nights till the end of time,
there you'll be, dominating the universe.*

Well, it's a nice way of
being remembered.

My nightmare is a serial. Part Four
is tonight.

How is it coming?

When it ended last time,
you were starting to stab me.

Pretty gruesome.

Well, it's a nightmare.

Of course I did do that
playfully at dinner last week.

I have to wonder...
how many episodes are still to come?

How did it start?

Part One began quietly...
you and I were casually conversing,
when suddenly you got that look
in your eye.

This look?

Please. Not while I'm awake.

Then what?

By the end of Part Two,
you were ridiculing my intellect.

Like my offhand remark a few days ago?
I was fooling around.

In Part Three it got vicious.
You questioned my manhood.

Like my humorous comment
late last evening?

You really said that?
I thought I was dreaming.

You did?

Do you mean to say
I'm <u>living</u> this nightmare?

If you're not too busy...
I think it's time we started Part Four.

*

And just why the nightmare at all?
Why isn't this perfect?

Something's not right.

And why not, I ask.

That's the question.

Here's the answer! You have no compassion!

Yes I do. The problem is...
it's not going to you.

And just who is it going to? No! Don't tell me!

I can't help it.
She preys on my mind.

That half a woman.

A magnificent half.

I want to know.
What was so magnificent about her?
That half?

Particular attributes.

What else?

The intimation...of what lay beyond.

Oh really? And just what did...lay beyond?

That's what I'm wondering.
That's what I'm dwelling on,
day and night. Week in, week out.
In fact, it's been years now...since
I first saw her there...half-hidden
in those shadows.

Truly pathetic.

Those garden shadows.

Those what?

Formed by those statues.

Statues of couples?
Shocking couples?

With flowers in their ears.

Beside a cafe...
a tiny cafe, covered with vines...?

The vines creeping over
a huge iron gate...

Outside the gate, a couple of lights...?

Lamppost lights,
which created the shadows.

The garden shadows.

So that...was you.

Out for a stroll,
after cake and champagne.
In the tiny cafe.

I was strolling there too.

And?

Those...attributes. The intimation...
of what lay beyond.

Well?

It's her. It's you.

And now what?

Now...now...for the very first time,
since it all began...I'm free!
Free to do this...throw my arms out,
right around you, and...

Well...no.

Excuse me? What...
what's the problem?

Oh I wouldn't call it a problem,
exactly. It's just that...well...

What?

I have to confess that...
the gentleman...
strolling there in the shadows...

Yes?

Well the truth of it is...
I regret to say this, I really do...but...
you're just half the man that <u>he</u> was.

I'll arrange that my tombstone
contain misinformation.

For what purpose?

I want to be remembered as somebody else.

Anyone in particular?

Someone whose dying is more tragic
than mine. When visitors come,
I want some real emotion out here,
not people just hanging around.

But then he'd be you.

I'll have to find someone who
agrees to that.

It may take a while. As a rule,
people like to be thought of
as being who they were.

What I'll need is a person
whose greatness lies in not caring
who he was.

Too bad that's not you.

Wait a minute. I've always
meant to be great somehow.

Maybe that's how.

What you're saying is, be
remembered as someone...
even if, it turns out,
that someone was me.

What could be greater?

I'll live forever
through the Digby Museum.

Exhibiting what?

Artifacts from my life.
First drafts of junk love letters...
a strand from my chest wig...
maybe a jar of my sparkling
bath water.

Who would be interested?

Students of humanity.
They'll see some rare evidence
of the sensuous life.

And what about my sensuous life?

I'm not sure it's museum material.

*Please. I'm at least as fascinating as you are,
and you know it!*

All right...
I'll set aside a large shelf.

That's hardly enough
for my self-portraits alone.

Maybe a corner gallery, then.

How about a space the same size as yours?

But...that would amount to
half of my life.

Appropriate, I'd say. Considering.

Considering what?

What you'd be without me.

It's just...well the name
of the place would no longer fit.

We'll give it a new name.

What, for example?

Something special. Something memorable.

Like what?

Maybe...the Museum of Digby and Marie.

Digby and Marie?

Well?

I'll have to admit...
it does have a ring to it.

And also a certain classical touch.

I just hope we're worthy of the name.